TEDDY BEARS'
Alphabet Soup

Verse by Jill Wolf
Illustrations by Katherine Gardner

Copyright © 1990 Antioch Publishing Company
ISBN 0-89954-550-5
Made in the United States of America

 Antioch Publishing Company
Yellow Springs, Ohio 45387

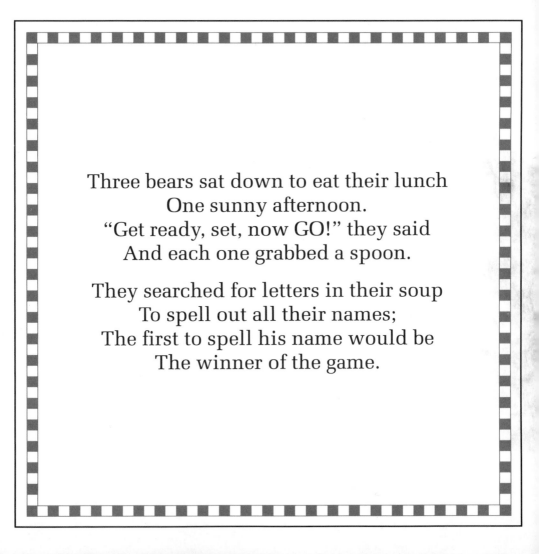

Three bears sat down to eat their lunch
One sunny afternoon.
"Get ready, set, now GO!" they said
And each one grabbed a spoon.

They searched for letters in their soup
To spell out all their names;
The first to spell his name would be
The winner of the game.

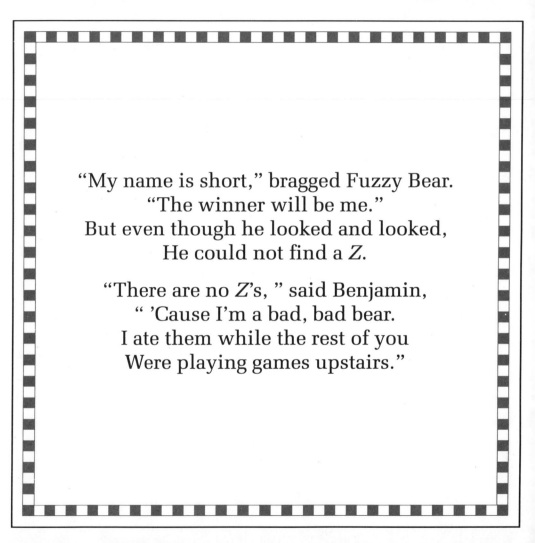

"My name is short," bragged Fuzzy Bear.
"The winner will be me."
But even though he looked and looked,
He could not find a *Z*.

"There are no *Z*'s, " said Benjamin,
" 'Cause I'm a bad, bad bear.
I ate them while the rest of you
Were playing games upstairs."

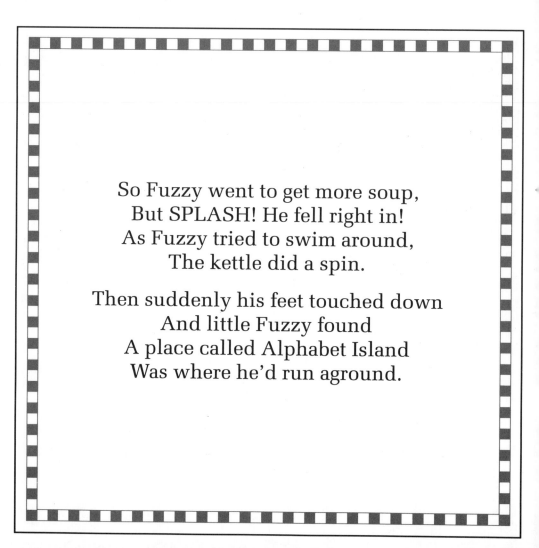

So Fuzzy went to get more soup,
But SPLASH! He fell right in!
As Fuzzy tried to swim around,
The kettle did a spin.

Then suddenly his feet touched down
And little Fuzzy found
A place called Alphabet Island
Was where he'd run aground.

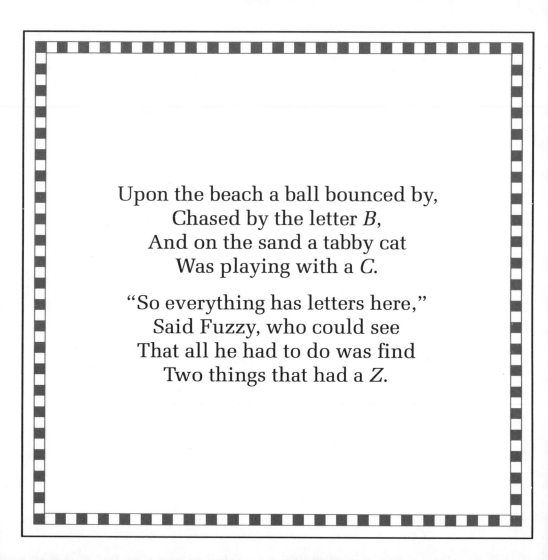

Upon the beach a ball bounced by,
Chased by the letter *B*,
And on the sand a tabby cat
Was playing with a *C*.

"So everything has letters here,"
Said Fuzzy, who could see
That all he had to do was find
Two things that had a *Z*.

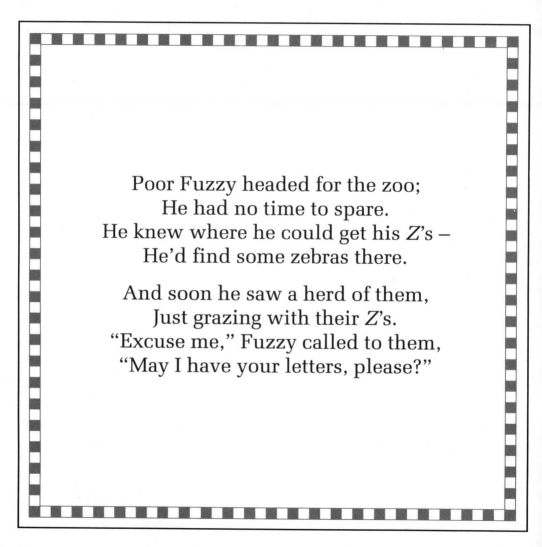

Poor Fuzzy headed for the zoo;
He had no time to spare.
He knew where he could get his *Z*'s –
He'd find some zebras there.

And soon he saw a herd of them,
Just grazing with their *Z*'s.
"Excuse me," Fuzzy called to them,
"May I have your letters, please?"

The zebras only shook their heads –
"We'd be 'ebras' without *Z*'s.
Whatever is an 'ebra' like?
Does it have stripes or speak Chinese?"

"I guess you're right," poor Fuzzy said.
"I never thought that far.
You'd better keep your letters then,
So you know what you are."

He sat upon a garden bench
And looked around the zoo;
He needed something with a *Z*.
What was Fuzzy going to do?

He tried to think of words with *Z*,
And then he heard a sound.
A bee flew in the flowerbeds;
A *B* chased it around.

Behind the bee there also flew
A little line of *Z*'s.
So Fuzzy spoke right up; he said,
"Mr. Bee, excuse me, please.

"Why is it that you have those *Z*'s
To follow you around?"
The bee replied, "The *Z*'s stand for
My special buzzing sound."

Then Fuzzy smiled and asked the bee,
"Could I have just two *Z*'s?
I wouldn't ask, except I must.
So may I have them, please?"

"Take two or twenty," said the bee.
"I'm always making more."
So Fuzzy caught a pair of *Z*'s
And hurried toward the shore.

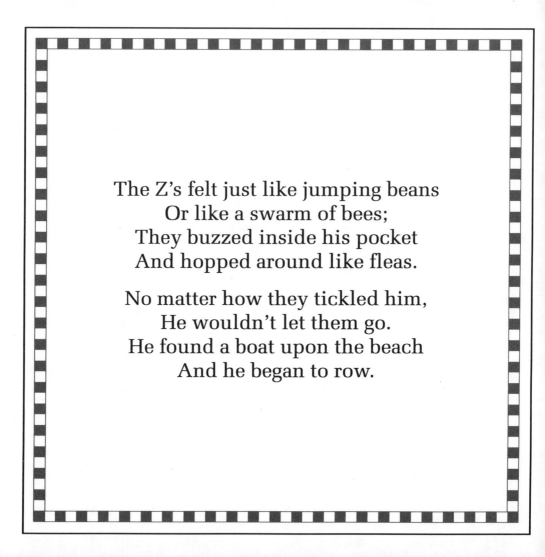

The Z's felt just like jumping beans
Or like a swarm of bees;
They buzzed inside his pocket
And hopped around like fleas.

No matter how they tickled him,
He wouldn't let them go.
He found a boat upon the beach
And he began to row.

He rowed and rowed across the sea
And came up through a hole,
Then climbed out of the kettle
And dropped the *Z*'s into his bowl.

So Fuzzy spelled his name out first
And finished up his soup.
He won the game although he had
To swim through slimy goop.

The
End